Bumble Bear
THE BEEGINNING

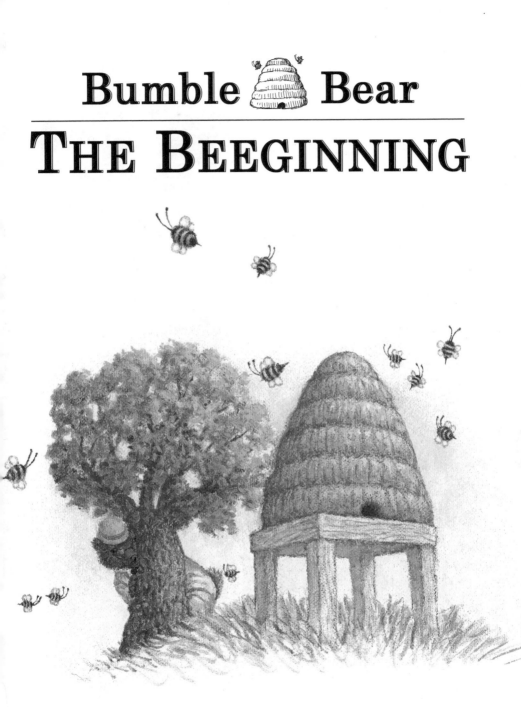

WRITTEN BY JAMES HOFFMAN
ILLUSTRATED BY JOHN SANFORD
EDITED BY SHANNON M. MULLALLY, Ph.D.

Bear loved honey. He loved honey more than any other bear could imagine loving it. He and his family lived in a cozy, little cottage on Honey Hill Farm that had shelves for honey and jam. But the honey jars on the shelves were usually empty, because Bear ate honey all day long.

And all day long he thought about getting *more* honey.
One day, a bee flew by, and a thought flew into Bear's
head. "Where bees *are*, honey *is*!"

He followed the bee to its hive. Then another idea came to Bear. "To get closer to the hive—to get the honey—I can dress like a bee."

He'd wear his striped pajamas! He'd hum a bee's buzz!
He'd pretend to fly! "And then, when the bees think I'm
just another big bee, I'll grab the honey!" he thought,
quickly changing clothes.

He finished his costume and spread his arms.
"I am Bumble Bear!" he shouted. And off he
dashed to the beehive.

As soon as he saw the hive, Bumble Bear became much too eager to put his paws on the honey. He forgot to hum or pretend to fly. He even forgot he was dressed like a bee. He wanted the honey so badly he made a beeline straight to the hive, crashing through the field, making more noise than a freight train.

Bumble Bear was so close to the hive, he could imagine reaching right inside for the honey. Then he stumbled!

He tripped and tumbled!

He was really flying through the air now! He knocked over the hive as he landed and combs of honey flew into the air, just out of reach.

And something else flew toward Bumble Bear—a swarm of angry bees. Bumble Bear had truly bumbled!

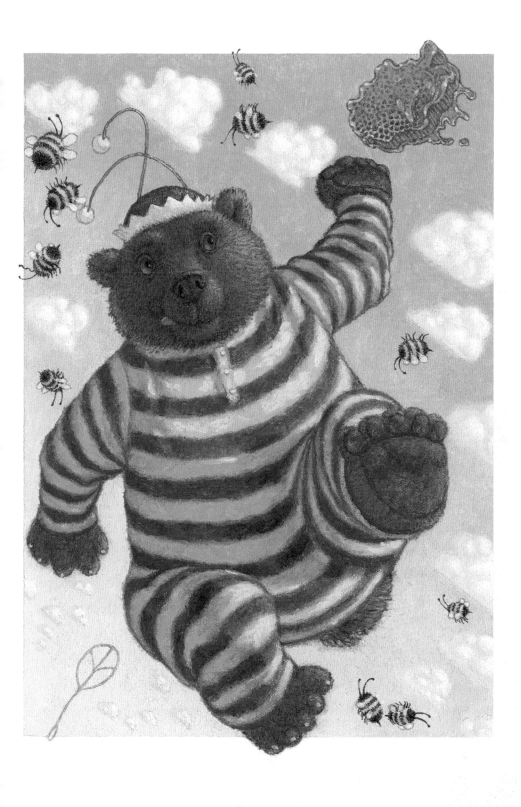

The bees aimed straight for the place where Bumble Bear's homemade stinger *used* to be. He felt stungled! He jumped into the water to get away from the bees. As a *Bee*ginner, he hadn't been able to get close to the honey in the hive.

When he landed in the pond, the cold water eased the hurt of his stings—but not his feelings. He'd lost his glasses. And he wore a hive on his head—a hive with no honey in it. "All this trouble and still no honey!" he thought. Bumble Bear had been humbled.

He grumbled as he trudged home in
his underwear. Home to empty jars.
Home to hungry Gwendolyn Bear,
his wife, and his two cubs, Wear
and Tear.

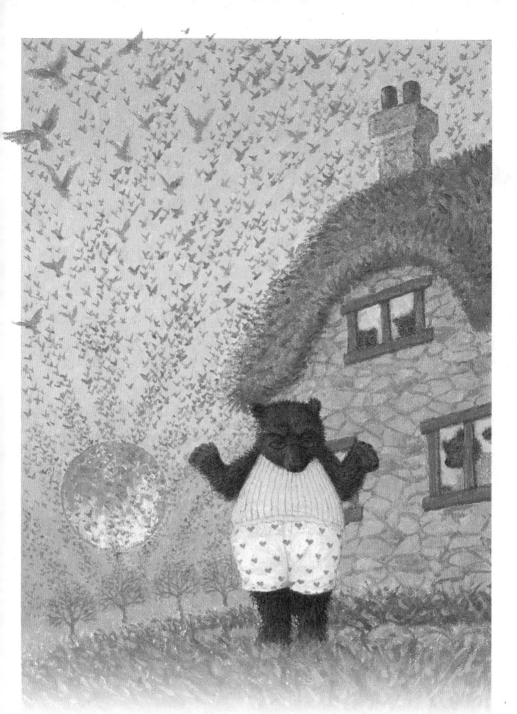

His stomach rumbled. It rumbled so loudly it scared
the birds. So loudly, in fact, that Wear and Tear and
Gwendolyn Bear heard him coming. They watched his
rumbling and grumbling from the cottage windows.

Upstairs, Gwendolyn tucked the cubs into bed. Tear said, "Daddy sure likes honey, but I like race cars."

"I like Pooh and honey, too," Wear said sleepily.

"I like a real honey,
and that's your father," said Gwendolyn Bear.
"He's a good bear but not a very good bee. Good night."

After his speech, Bumble Bear went to
his study and planned far into the night,
thinking up new ways to get honey into
his rumbling tummy.

"Tomorrow I'll try again," he mumbled. "What if..."

That night, Bumble Bear lectured to Wear and Tear on the value of honey as he peered into the depths of an empty jar. Wear and Tear and Gwendolyn Bear were used to this lecture. They'd heard it all before.